FIVE
FAVOURITE
STORYTIME
TALES

All Ladybird books are available at most bookshops,
supermarkets and newsagents, or can be ordered direct from:
Ladybird Postal Sales
PO Box 133 Paignton TQ3 2YP England
Telephone: (+44) 01803 554761
Fax: (+44) 01803 663394

A catalogue record for this book is available
from the British Library

Published by Ladybird Books Ltd
A subsidiary of the Penguin Group
A Pearson Company
© LADYBIRD BOOKS LTD MCMXCVIII
Stories in this book were previously published by Ladybird Books Ltd
in the *Favourite Tales* series.

LADYBIRD and the device of a Ladybird are trademarks of
Ladybird Books Ltd Loughborough Leicestershire UK

FIVE
FAVOURITE
STORYTIME
TALES

Ladybird

Introduction

Children will treasure this collection of timeless storytime tales. The easy-to-read retellings, enhanced by exciting, richly colourful illustrations, faithfully capture all the magic of the original stories.

Contents

Chicken Licken

Based on a traditional folk tale
retold by Joan Stimson
Illustrated by Petula Stone

Tom Thumb

Based on the story by
Jacob and Wilhelm Grimm
retold by Audrey Daly
Illustrated by Peter Stevenson

Cover and Borders illustrated by
Peter Stevenson

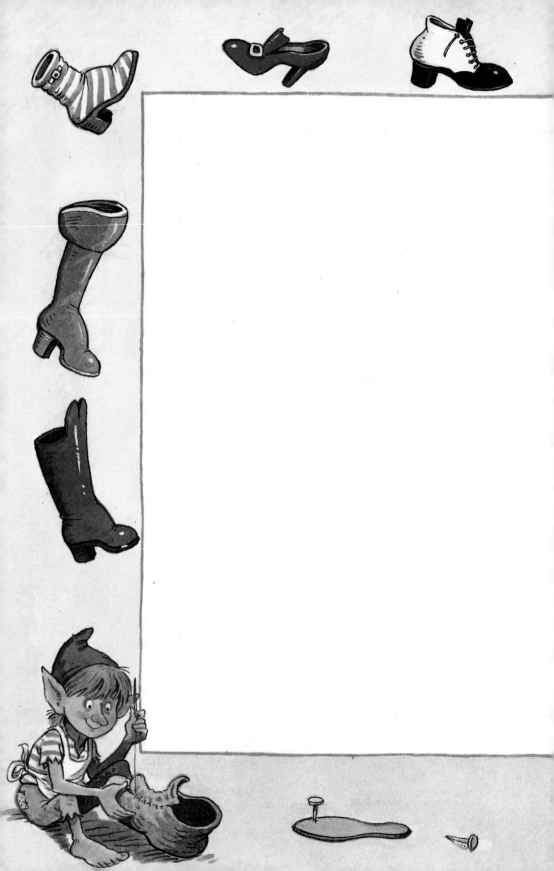

The Elves
and the
Shoemaker

Once upon a time there was a poor shoemaker who had no money left to buy food for himself and his wife. When he looked round his shop, he found that all he had was just enough leather to make one pair of shoes.

As he carefully cut out the shoes, he wondered sadly if anyone would ever come along to buy them. Then he laid out the leather on his workbench, ready to sew the next day, and went upstairs to bed.

In the morning, when he went to his workbench, the shoemaker couldn't believe his eyes. Instead of the leather he had cut out the night before, he saw a pair of fine shoes, already made.

The shoemaker looked carefully at the shoes. The stitches were small and even, and the shoes had been polished until they shone. He was very puzzled and showed them to his wife. Who could have made the shoes so perfectly?

Later that day, a rich woman came into the shop to buy some shoes. When the shoemaker showed her the pair he had found on his workbench, the woman smiled.

"These are very fine shoes," she said as she tried them on. "They fit perfectly. I'll give you five pieces of silver for them."

Now the shoemaker could buy some food, and he could also buy enough · leather for *two* pairs of shoes.

As before, he cut out the leather and went to bed.

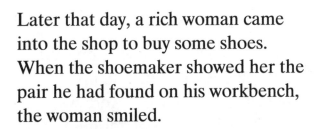

Once again, the same thing happened. When the shoemaker went to his workbench next day, there were two pairs of fine shoes waiting for him.

They were polished so that they glowed in the sunlight, and the stitches were small and even.

That afternoon, a rich merchant came into the shop. He liked the shoes so much that he bought *both* pairs, and he paid the shoemaker well for them.

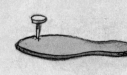

That day, the shoemaker was able to buy enough leather for *four* pairs of shoes. Just as before, he cut out the leather and left it on his workbench overnight. And in the morning he found four fine pairs of shoes there instead.

The same thing happened night after night. And day after day, rich people came to buy the shoes. Soon the shoemaker and his wife were rich too.

One evening, not long before Christmas, the shoemaker said to his wife, "Someone has been helping us all this time, sewing the shoes so beautifully, and we still don't know who it is. How can we find out?"

"Well," said his wife, "why don't we stay up tonight and watch?"

So after dinner, they lit a candle and went into the shop. They hid behind the counter and waited to see what would happen.

At last the door opened and in ran
two tiny elves, dressed in rags. They
went straight to the workbench,
picked up the leather lying there, and
set to work.

They sewed and hammered until all
the shoes were finished. And they
polished every shoe until it shone in
the moonlight. Then they ran quickly
away.

The next morning, the shoemaker said to his wife, "Those elves have been working so hard for us. How can we ever repay them?"

"I know!" said his wife. "Why don't we make them something warm to wear? Their own clothes were thin and torn, and their little feet were bare. I could start by knitting them little caps, and you could make them some shoes."

The shoemaker thought that was a
very good idea. That evening, he
carefully made two pairs of tiny shoes,
and his wife knitted two little caps.

Over the next few days, the
shoemaker helped his wife to make
all sorts of clothes for the elves. They
made some little shirts, trousers and
waistcoats. Finally, the shoemaker's
wife knitted two tiny pairs of socks.

By Christmas Eve, everything stood ready in a little pile. The shoemaker's wife fetched some pretty paper and ribbons, and they wrapped each present one by one.

The shoemaker was so pleased with the little shoes he had made that he saved them till last, and wrapped them up very carefully.

Then they put all the presents out on the workbench, and hid behind the counter to wait for the elves.

In the middle of the night the elves dashed in, ready to start work. But when they went to the workbench, all they found there was the little pile of presents.

The elves looked at each other in surprise. Then they realised that the presents were for them, and they laughed and began to unwrap the packages.

When they saw the clothes, they leapt with joy. They took off all their ragged things and put on their brand new outfits.

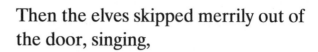

Then the elves skipped merrily out of the door, singing,

"Oh what handsome boys we are!
We will work on shoes no more!"

That was the last the shoemaker and his wife saw of the two little men. But they never forgot the elves, and they were rich and happy for the rest of their lives.

Puss
in Boots

Once upon a time there was a miller who had three sons. When the miller died, he left the mill to his eldest son and a donkey to his second son. They were able to set to work straightaway.

But all that was left for the youngest son was his father's cat.

"Poor Puss," said the miller's son.
"How shall we manage?"

"Don't worry," said the cat. "Give me
a pair of boots and a bag and we will
do very well together."

When the miller's son brought the
things the cat wanted, Puss got ready.
He put on his boots and left the bag,
filled with lettuce leaves, in a field.

Very soon, a little rabbit came to
nibble the lettuce.

Quick as a flash, Puss caught the rabbit in his bag and carried it to the King's palace.

"Your Majesty," said Puss, "please accept this fine rabbit as a present from my master, the Marquis of Carrabas."

"I've never heard of him," said the King, "but you deserve a treat from the kitchen."

The next day, Puss heard that the King and his daughter would be driving by the river.

"Master," he said, "do what I say and we shall be rich. You must take off your clothes and swim in the river. And you must believe that your name is the Marquis of Carrabas."

"I've never heard of him," said the miller's son, "but I'll do as you say, Puss."

Before long, the King drove past with his daughter, the Princess. He was pleased to see Puss again.

"Your Majesty," said Puss, bowing low, "a very terrible thing has happened. My master, the Marquis of Carrabas, was swimming in the river when some thieves came and stole all his clothes!"

"How dreadful!" exclaimed the King and the Princess together.

The King sent off to the palace at once for some clothes. When the miller's son put them on, he looked very handsome.

"Please come and ride in our carriage," said the King. "May I present my daughter?"

Puss ran quickly on ahead. When he saw some men making hay in a field, he shouted to them, "The King is coming. If he asks, you must say that this land belongs to the Marquis of Carrabas."

"We've never heard of him," said the
haymakers, "but we'll do as you say."

Soon the King drove past in his carriage with the Princess and the miller's son. "Tell me, my man," said the King to a haymaker, "whose land is this?"

"It belongs to the Marquis of Carrabas, Your Majesty," the man replied at once.

Meanwhile, Puss had found out that
the land was really owned by an ogre
who lived in a huge castle nearby.

Puss quickly made his way to the
castle and knocked on the door.
"Sir, is it true that you are a very
good magician?" he asked the ogre.

The ogre, who liked to show off, replied, "Yes, it's true. I can even turn myself into a lion!"

Quick as a flash, the ogre became a fierce, roaring lion!

Puss was so startled that he scrambled
to the top of a chest of drawers to
hide.

When the ogre had changed himself
back again, Puss jumped down.
"Turning into a lion must be easy for
someone as big and strong as you," he
said. "But can you turn yourself into
something *tiny* – like a mouse?"

"Of course I can!" roared the ogre.
"Just watch!"

In the blink of an eye, the ogre
became a little mouse scurrying across
the floor. Puss instantly
pounced on him and
ate him up.

"Now that the ogre is gone," Puss said
to himself, "this castle will make a
very fine home for my master, the
Marquis of Carrabas."

The King was most impressed by the handsome young man who owned such rich land and lived in such a magnificent castle. "He would make a fine husband for my daughter," the King said.

So the miller's son and the Princess and Puss lived happily ever after. And now *everyone* has heard of the Marquis of Carrabas!

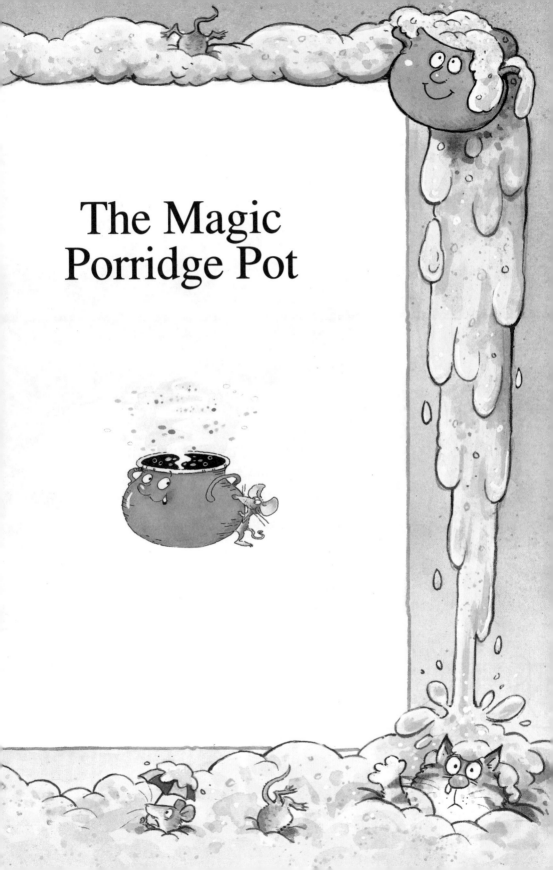

The Magic
Porridge Pot

Once upon a time, there was a little
girl who lived with her widowed
mother. They were very poor,
and one day they had nothing
left to eat at all.

The little girl was so hungry that she
ran into the woods and began to cry.

"Whatever is the matter?" asked a
kind voice.

The kind voice belonged to an old woman. When she heard how hungry the little girl was, she gave her a magic cooking pot.

"Just say the words, 'Cook, little pot, cook!'" she explained, "and it will give you lovely, hot porridge.

"But once the porridge is cooked, you must say, 'Stop, little pot, stop!'"

The little girl spoke to the pot right away. "Cook, little pot, cook!" she said, and to her surprise, it began to bubble!

The porridge smelled wonderful. As soon as it was cooked, the little girl said, "Stop, little pot, stop!"

Then she ate up every last bit!

The little girl ran all the way home.
She showed her mother the magic
cooking pot and told her what the old
woman had said.

Her mother was delighted.

"All our troubles are over," she cried.

And she was right. Because, whenever the little girl and her mother were hungry, all they had to say was, "Cook, little pot, cook!"

Each time, the magic pot would cook them some lovely, hot porridge.

The little girl and her mother could hardly believe how lucky they were.

One day the little girl went out for a walk. While she was away, her mother felt hungry, so she picked up the magic pot.

"Cook, little pot, cook!" she said, and the pot set to work. The mother was soon so busy eating that she forgot to tell the pot to stop!

On and on cooked the pot. Soon the porridge began to spill over the top.

As soon as the mother saw what was happening, she knew that she must tell the pot to stop cooking.

But she had forgotten the words!

On and on cooked the magic pot.
First the porridge covered the kitchen
table. Then it spread across the floor.
Soon the *whole house* was full of
porridge.

The porridge spilled into the street
and filled all the other houses. Then it
began to ooze along other streets.

And still the magic pot went on
cooking!

By now the town was beginning to *drown* in porridge. The people started to panic. They ran out of their porridge-filled houses and into the porridge-filled streets.

"Help!" cried the mother. "I must stop the magic cooking pot, but I can't remember the words."

"Help!" cried the townspeople. "Soon the whole *world* will be filled with porridge!"

Just as the porridge reached the last house in the town, the little girl came back from her walk. She could hardly believe her eyes.

"*Please* tell the magic pot to stop making porridge," begged her mother.

The little girl took hold of the magic pot and said sternly, "Stop, little pot, STOP!"

And, at last, the magic pot stopped cooking porridge.

The whole town breathed a sigh of relief. It hadn't drowned in porridge after all.

But, if ever you visit there, be prepared… for porridge, porridge and *more porridge*!

TONI'S
MENU
LARGE PORRIDGE
2.00
SMALL PORRIDGE
1.00
MED PORRIDGE
1.50
EXTRAS...
BOWL 10p SPOON 5p

Chicken
Licken

Once upon a time there was a little chick called Chicken Licken.

One day, as he was playing, an acorn fell on his head.

"Help!" thought Chicken Licken. "The sky is falling down!"

And he ran off to tell the King.

On the way, Chicken Licken met Henny Penny.

"Oh! Henny Penny!" cried Chicken Licken. "The sky is falling down and I'm off to tell the King."

"Then I shall come too," said Henny Penny.

So Chicken Licken and Henny Penny hurried off to find the King.

On the way, Chicken Licken and
Henny Penny met Cocky Locky.

"Oh! Cocky Locky!" cried Chicken
Licken. "The sky is falling down and
we're off to tell the King."

"Then I shall come too," said Cocky
Locky.

So Chicken Licken, Henny Penny and Cocky Locky hurried off to find the King.

On the way, Chicken Licken, Henny Penny and Cocky Locky met Ducky Lucky.

"Oh! Ducky Lucky!" cried Chicken Licken. "The sky is falling down and we're off to tell the King."

"Then I shall come too," said Ducky Lucky.

So Chicken Licken, Henny Penny,
Cocky Locky and Ducky Lucky
hurried off to find the King.

On the way, Chicken Licken, Henny Penny, Cocky Locky and Ducky Lucky met Drakey Lakey.

"Oh! Drakey Lakey!" cried Chicken Licken. "The sky is falling down and we're off to tell the King."

"Then I shall come too," said Drakey Lakey.

So Chicken Licken, Henny Penny, Cocky Locky, Ducky Lucky and Drakey Lakey hurried off to find the King.

On the way, Chicken Licken, Henny Penny, Cocky Locky, Ducky Lucky and Drakey Lakey met Goosey Loosey.

"Oh! Goosey Loosey!" cried Chicken Licken. "The sky is falling down and we're off to tell the King."

"Then I shall come too," said Goosey Loosey.

So Chicken Licken, Henny Penny,
Cocky Locky, Ducky Lucky, Drakey
Lakey and Goosey Loosey hurried off
to find the King.

On the way, Chicken Licken, Henny Penny, Cocky Locky, Ducky Lucky, Drakey Lakey and Goosey Loosey met Turkey Lurkey.

"Oh! Turkey Lurkey!" cried Chicken Licken. "The sky is falling down and we're off to tell the King."

"Then I shall come too," said Turkey Lurkey.

So Chicken Licken, Henny Penny, Cocky Locky, Ducky Lucky, Drakey Lakey, Goosey Loosey and Turkey Lurkey hurried off to find the King.

But on the way, they met Foxy Loxy!

"Good morning," said Foxy Loxy. "Where are you all going in such a hurry?"

"Oh! Foxy Loxy!" cried Chicken Licken. "The sky is falling down and we're off to tell the King."

"Follow me," said Foxy Loxy. "I know just where to find the King."

So Chicken Licken, Henny Penny, Cocky Locky, Ducky Lucky, Drakey Lakey, Goosey Loosey and Turkey Lurkey all followed Foxy Loxy.

But he didn't take them to the King.
He led them straight to his den,
where his wife and all the little foxes
were waiting for their dinner.

Then the foxes ate up Chicken
Licken, Henny Penny, Cocky Locky,
Ducky Lucky, Drakey Lakey, Goosey
Loosey and Turkey Lurkey.

And Chicken Licken never did find the King to tell him that the sky was falling down!

Tom
Thumb

There was once a woodsman and his wife who were very sad because they had no children.

"If only we had a child to love," said the wife, "I wouldn't mind if he were as small as my thumb!"

Time passed and at last they had a son, which made them both very happy.

Strangely enough, the boy never grew any bigger than a man's thumb, and so they called him "Tom Thumb".

One day, as Tom's father set off for work, he sighed, "If only Tom were bigger, he could drive the cart into the forest for me."

Tom looked at his mother. "I can do it anyway!" he said. "If you will harness the horse, Mother, I'll show you how." Tom's mother did as he asked.

"Now put me in the horse's ear," said Tom. "I'll tell him which way to go."

So off went the cart with Tom tucked in the horse's ear. When Tom said, "Turn left," or "Turn right," the horse did just that.

Two men, who were walking in the forest, were surprised to see a horse and cart going along without a driver. They followed the cart to see where it went.

When the cart stopped, the two men were amazed to see Tom's father lift him down from the horse's ear.

"What a clever little fellow that is," said one of the men. "Will you sell him to us?"

"I would never sell him," said the woodsman proudly. "He is my son."

But Tom whispered, "Go on, Father, let me go with them. It will be an adventure, and I know I can get home soon."

The woodsman didn't want to, but at last he sold Tom for a lot of money.

One of the men put Tom in his pocket, saying, "We can put him on show in the towns. He is going to make us rich!" Then they set off.

Towards evening, Tom called out, "Please put me down so that I can stretch my legs."

When the men put him down, Tom ran straight off and hid. The men looked everywhere, but he had disappeared.

Tom looked for somewhere safe
to sleep. He soon found an empty
snail shell and curled up inside it.
Just as he was falling asleep, he
heard voices nearby.

Two thieves were talking. "We'll
sneak into the parson's house and
steal his money!" said one.

"Take me with you," said Tom in a
loud voice. "I can help you!"

The men were puzzled. They could
hear a voice, but they couldn't see
anyone. They were astonished
when they found the tiny boy.

"I can get in through a crack in the window," said Tom, "and I can throw the money down to you."

The men agreed to take Tom with them and see what he could do.

When they got to the parson's house, Tom did as he had said. Then, standing on the window ledge, he shouted, "Do you want *all* the money that's here?"

"Sssh!" said the thieves, frightened. "You'll wake the whole house!"

But Tom shouted even louder.
"HOW MUCH MONEY
SHOULD I THROW DOWN?"

The noise woke the cook, who
was sleeping in the next room.

While the cook got up to look around, Tom ran off to the barn. There he settled down to sleep in the hay.

By the time the cook got downstairs, the thieves had run away and there was no sign of Tom at all.

Next morning the cook went to
milk and feed the cow. She picked
up the very bundle of hay that
Tom was sleeping in.

Tom woke up to find himself
being tossed up and down in the
cow's mouth. He landed in the
cow's stomach with all the hay.

"Stop eating!" yelled Tom. "I'm
getting smothered!"

The cook was so startled to hear a
voice coming from the cow's mouth
that she ran to the parson.
"Help!" she cried.
"The cow's
talking!"

"Don't be silly," said the parson. "Cows don't talk."

Just then Tom shouted again – the parson was astonished.

As soon as he could, Tom crawled out of the cow's stomach and slipped away. No one saw him go.

But Tom's troubles were far from over. A hungry wolf was passing by and saw Tom in the farmyard.

"This will make a tasty little snack," thought the wolf, and he swallowed Tom in one gulp.

Clever Tom quickly thought of a plan. "Wolf," he called, "if you are still hungry, I know where there is lots of food." And he told the wolf how to get to his very own house, which was not far away.

When they got there, Tom said, "Just crawl through the drain and you'll be in the kitchen, where there is always plenty to eat."

The drain was quite small, but the wolf squeezed and pushed and *just* managed to get through.

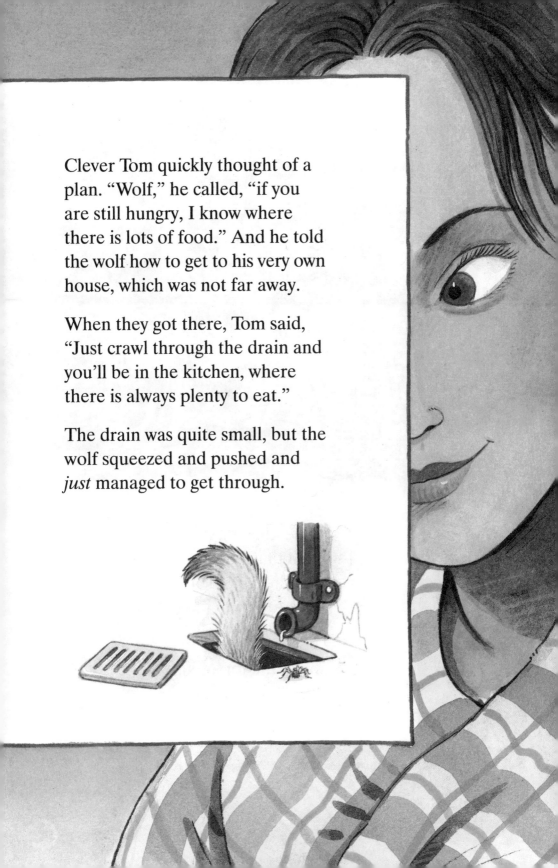

In the kitchen, the wolf ate so much that when he tried to crawl back through the drain, he was much too fat!

Then Tom began to shout and sing at the top of his voice.

His parents came to the kitchen
door to see what all the noise was
about.

"It's a wolf!" said Tom's father.
"Where's my axe?"

"Wait, Father!" shouted Tom.
"It's me! I'm here, inside the
wolf's stomach!"

"Tom!" cried his father. "Don't worry, we'll save you!"

Tom's father picked up his axe and hit the wolf over the head. Then, very carefully, he cut a little hole in the wolf's stomach.

Out jumped Tom, safe and sound. "I told you I'd be back soon, Father!" he laughed.

Tom's parents were overjoyed to see him. "We'll never part with you again," said his father, "not for all the money in the world."

"And I will never leave home again," promised Tom. "I've had enough adventures to last a lifetime!"